# THE REAL
# MOTHER GOOSE

**SEE-SAW**

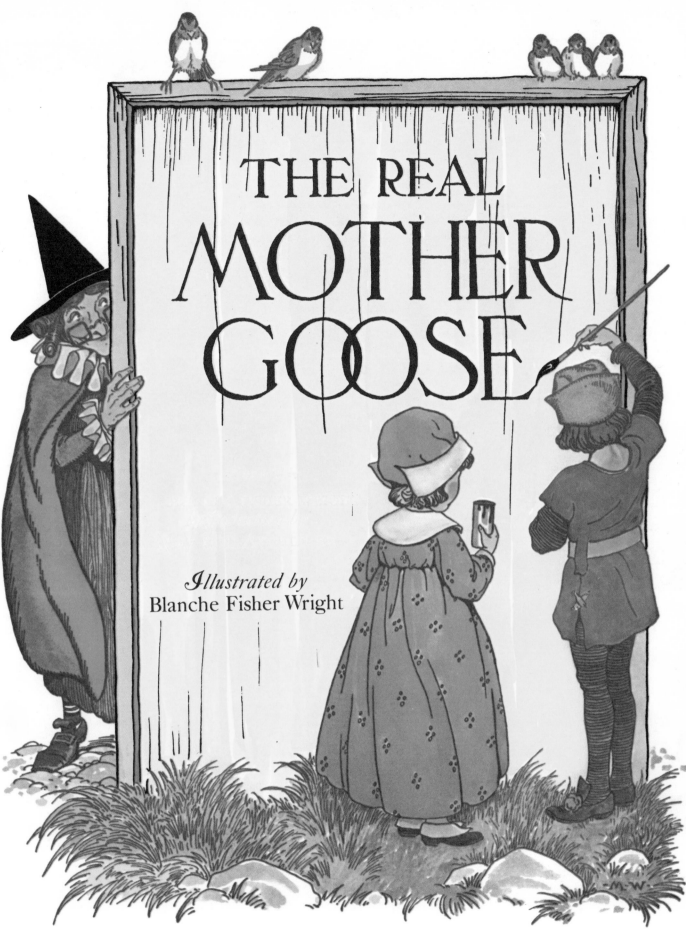

# THE REAL
# MOTHER
# GOOSE

*Illustrated by*
Blanche Fisher Wright

# RAND McNALLY & CO. CHICAGO

Printed in U. S. A.

First printing, 1916
Second printing, 1917
Third printing, 1918
Fourth printing, 1919
Fifth printng, 1920
Sixth printing, 1921
Seventh printing, 1922
Eighth printing, 1923
Ninth printing, 1924
Tenth printing, 1925
Eleventh printing, 1926
Twelfth printing, 1927
Thirteenth printing, 1928
Fourteenth printing, 1930
Fifteenth printing, 1931
Sixteenth printing, 1932
Seventeenth printing, July, 1934
Eighteenth printing, April, 1935
Nineteenth printing, September, 1936
Twentieth printing, December, 1938
Twenty-first printing, March, 1940
Twenty-second printing, February, 1941
Twenty-third printing, August, 1941
Twenty-fourth printing, August, 1942
Twenty-fifth printing, January, 1943
Twenty-sixth printing, March, 1944
Twenty-seventh printing, November, 1944
Twenty-eighth printing, June, 1945
Twenty-ninth printing, December, 1945
Thirtieth printing, June, 1946
Thirty-first printing, May, 1948
Thirty-second printing, January, 1950
Thirty-third printing, March, 1951
Thirty-fourth printing, January, 1952
Thirty-fifth printing, December, 1952
Thirty-sixth printing, December, 1953
Thirty-seventh printing, December, 1954
Thirty-eighth printing, October, 1956
Thirty-ninth printing, May, 1957
Fortieth printing, October, 1958
Forty-first printing, June, 1960
Forty-second printing, January, 1961
Forty-third printing, January, 1962
Forty-fourth printing, Febuary, 1963
Forty-fifth printing, October, 1963
Forty-sixth printing, May, 1964
Forty-seventh printing, January, 1965
Forty-eighth printing, September, 1965
Forty-ninth printing, April, 1966
Fiftieth printing, May, 1966
Fifty-first printing, July, 1967
Fifty-second printing, May, 1968
Fifty-third printing, July, 1969
Fifty-fourth printing, August, 1970
Fifty-fifth printing, July, 1971
Fifty-sixth printing, October, 1971
Fifty-seventh printing, October, 1972
Fifty-eighth printing, January, 1973
Fifty-ninth printing, October, 1973
Sixtieth printing, March, 1974
Sixty-first printing, July, 1974
Sixty-second printing, November, 1974
Sixty-third printing, July, 1975
Sixty-fourth printing, October, 1975
Sixty-fifth printing, June, 1976

# A LIST OF THE RHYMES

*(For an alphabetical list of first lines see pp. 7-9)*

Little Bo-Peep
Little Boy Blue
Rain
The Clock
Winter
Fingers and Toes
A Seasonable Song
Dame Trot and Her Cat
Three Children on the Ice
Cross Patch
The Old Woman Under a Hill
Tweedle-Dum and Tweedle-Dee
Oh Dear!
Old Mother Goose
Little Jumping Joan
Pat-a-Cake
Money and the Mare
Robin Redbreast
A Melancholy Song
Jack
Going to St. Ives
Thirty Days Hath September
Baby Dolly
Bees
Come Out to Play
If Wishes Were Horses
To Market
Old Chairs to Mend
Robin and Richard
A Man and a Maid
Here Goes My Lord
The Clever Hen
Two Birds
Leg Over Leg
Lucy Locket
When Jenny Wren Was Young
Barber
The Flying Pig
Solomon Grundy
Hush-a-Bye
Burnie Bee
Three Wise Men of Gotham
The Hunter of Reigate
Little Polly Flinders
Ride Away, Ride Away
Pippen Hill
Pussy-Cat and Queen
The Winds
Clap Handies
Christmas
Elizabeth

Just Like Me
Play Days
Heigh-Ho, the Carrion Crow
A B C
A Needle and Thread
Banbury Cross
The Man in Our Town
Georgy Porgy
For Every Evil
Cushy Cow
Wee Willie Winkie
About the Bush
See-Saw
Robin-a-Bobbin
John Smith
Simple Simon
Three Blind Mice
Five Toes
A Little Man
Doctor Foster
Diddle Diddle Dumpling
Jerry Hall
Lengthening Days
The Black Hen
The Mist
A Candle
Miss Muffet
Curly-Locks
Humpty Dumpty
One, Two, Three
The Dove and the Wren
Master I Have
Pins
Shall We Go A-Shearing?
Goosey, Goosey, Gander
Old Mother Hubbard
The Cock and the Hen
Blue Bell Boy
Why May Not I Love Johnny?
Jack Jelf
Jack Sprat
Hush-a-Bye
Daffodils
The Girl in the Lane
Hush-a-Bye
Nancy Dawson
Handy Pandy
Jack and Jill
The Alphabet
Dance to Your Daddie
One Misty Moisty Morning

Robin Hood and Little John
Rain
The Old Woman from France
Teeth and Gums
The Robins
The Old Man
T'Other Little Tune
My Kitten
If All the Seas Were One Sea
Pancake Day
A Plum Pudding
Forehead, Eyes, Cheeks, Nose, etc.
Two Pigeons
A Sure Test
Lock and Key
The Lion and the Unicorn
The Merchants of London
I Had a Little Husband
To Babylon
I'll Tell You a Story
A Strange Old Woman
Sleep, Baby, Sleep
Cry, Baby
Baa, Baa, Black Sheep
Little Fred
The Cat and the Fiddle
Doctor Fell
A Counting-Out Rhyme
Jack and His Fiddle
Buttons
Hot Boiled Beans
Little Pussy
Sing a Song of Sixpence
Tommy Tittlemouse
The Derby Ram
The Hobby-Horse
The Mulberry Bush
Young Lambs to Sell
Boy and the Sparrow
Old Woman, Old Woman
The First of May
Sulky Sue
The House That Jack Built
Saturday, Sunday
Little Jenny Wren
The Old Woman and the Pedlar
Bobby Snooks
The Little Moppet
I Saw a Ship A-Sailing
A Walnut
The Man in the Moon

# A LIST OF THE RHYMES—Continued

One, He Loves
Bat, Bat
Hark! Hark!
The Hart
My Love
The Man of Bombay
Poor Old Robinson Crusoe!
A Sieve
My Maid Mary
A Difficult Rhyme
Pretty John Watts
Good Advice
I Love Sixpence
Bye, Baby Bunting
Tom, Tom, the Piper's Son
Comical Folk
Cock-Crow
Tommy Snooks
The Three Sons
The Blacksmith
Two Gray Kits
One, Two, Buckle My Shoe
Cock-a-Doodle-Do!
Pairs or Pears
Belleisle
Old King Cole
See, See
Dapple-Gray
A Well
Coffee and Tea
Pussy-Cat Mew
The Little Girl with a Curl
Dreams
A Cock and Bull Story
For Baby
Myself
Over the Water
Candle-Saving
Fears and Tears
The Kilkenny Cats
Old Grimes
A Week of Birthdays
A Chimney
Ladybird
The Man Who Had Naught
The Tailors and the Snail
Around the Green Gravel
Intery, Mintery
Caesar's Song
As I Was Going Along
Hector Protector
Billy, Billy
Rock-a-Bye, Baby
The Man in the Wilderness
Little Jack Horner
The Bird Scarer
Mary, Mary, Quite Contrary

Bessy Bell and Mary Gray
Needles and Pins
Pussy-Cat and the Dumplings
Dance, Thumbkin, Dance
Mary's Canary
The Little Bird
Birds of a Feather
The Dusty Miller
A Star
The Greedy Man
The Ten O'Clock Scholar
Cock-a-Doodle-Do
An Icicle
A Ship's Nail
The Old Woman of Leeds
The Boy in the Barn
Sunshine
Willy, Willy
Tongs
Jack Jingle
The Quarrel
The Pumpkin-Eater
Shoeing
Betty Blue
That's All
Bedtime
Dance, Little Baby
My Little Maid
For Want of a Nail
Pease Porridge
Ring a Ring o' Roses
The Crooked Sixpence
This Is the Way
Ducks and Drakes
The Donkey
If
The Bells
Little Girl and Queen
The King of France
Peter Piper
One to Ten
An Equal
The Tarts
Come, Let's to Bed
Little Maid
What Are Little Boys Made Of?
Bandy Legs
The Girl and the Birds
A Pig
Jenny Wren
Little Tom Tucker
Where Are You Going, My Pretty
    Maid?
The Old Woman of Gloucester
Multiplication Is Vexation
Little King Boggen
Whistle

Bell Horses
Taffy
The Robin
The Old Woman of Harrow
Young Roger and Dolly
The Piper and His Cow
The Man of Derby
The Coachman
There was an Old Woman
A Thorn
The Old Woman of Surrey
The Little Mouse
Boy and Girl
When
Sing, Sing
London Bridge
March Winds
The Balloon
A Cherry
The Lost Shoe
Hot Codlins
Swan
Three Straws
The Man of Tobago
Ding, Dong, Bell
A Sunshiny Shower
The Farmer and the Raven
Christmas
Willy Boy
Polly and Sukey
The Death and Burial of Poor Cock
    Robin
The Mouse and the Clock
Hot-Cross Buns
Bobby Shaftoe
The Bunch of Blue Ribbons
The Woman of Exeter
Sneezing
Pussy-Cat by the Fire
When the Snow Is on the Ground

# AN ALPHABETICAL LIST OF FIRST LINES

# AN ALPHABETICAL LIST OF FIRST LINES—Continued

# AN ALPHABETICAL LIST OF FIRST LINES—Continued

9

RAIN

# THE REAL
# MOTHER GOOSE

## LITTLE BO-PEEP

Little Bo-Peep has lost her sheep,
    And can't tell where to find
        them;
Leave them alone, and they'll come
        home,
    And bring their tails behind
        them.

Little Bo-Peep fell fast asleep,
    And dreamt she heard them
        bleating;
But when she awoke, she found it
        a joke,
    For still they all were fleeting.

Then up she took her little crook,
    Determined for to find them;
She found them indeed, but it made
        her heart bleed,
    For they'd left all their tails
        behind 'em!

It happened one day, as Bo-peep
        did stray
    Unto a meadow hard by—

There she espied their tails, side
        by side,
    All hung on a tree to dry.

She heaved a sigh and wiped her eye,
    And over the hillocks she
        raced;
And tried what she could, as a
        shepherdess should,
    That each tail should be prop-
        erly placed.

## LITTLE BOY BLUE

Little Boy Blue, come, blow your
        horn!
The sheep's in the meadow, the
        cow's in the corn.
Where's the little boy that looks
        after the sheep?
Under the haystack, fast asleep!

## RAIN

Rain, rain, go away,
Come again another day;
Little Johnny wants to play.

## FINGERS AND TOES

Every lady in this land
Has twenty nails, upon each
    hand
Five, and twenty on hands and
    feet:
All this is true, without deceit

## A SEASONABLE SONG

Piping hot, smoking hot.
    What I've got
    You have not.
Hot gray pease, hot, hot, hot;
Hot gray pease, hot.

## THE CLOCK

There's a neat little clock,—
    In the schoolroom it stands,—
And it points to the time
    With its two little hands.

And may we, like the clock,
    Keep a face clean and bright,
With hands ever ready
    To do what is right.

## WINTER

Cold and raw the north wind
    doth blow,
Bleak in the morning early;
All the hills are covered with
    snow,
And winter's now come fairly.

## DAME TROT AND HER CAT

Dame Trot and her cat
Led a peaceable life,
When they were not troubled
With other folks' strife.

When Dame had her dinner
Pussy would wait,
And was sure to receive
A nice piece from her plate.

## THREE CHILDREN ON THE ICE

Three children sliding on the ice
Upon a summer's day,
As it fell out, they all fell in,
The rest they ran away.

Oh, had these children been at
school,
Or sliding on dry ground,
Ten thousand pounds to one penny
They had not then been drowned.

Ye parents who have children dear,
And ye, too, who have none,
If you would keep them safe abroad
Pray keep them safe at home.

## CROSS PATCH

Cross patch, draw the latch,
Sit by the fire and spin;
Take a cup and drink it up,
Then call your neighbors in.

## THE OLD WOMAN UNDER A HILL

There was an old woman
Lived under a hill;
And if she's not gone,
She lives there still.

## TWEEDLE-DUM AND TWEEDLE-DEE

Tweedle-dum and Tweedle-dee
Resolved to have a battle,
For Tweedle-dum said Tweedle-dee
Had spoiled his nice new rattle.

Just then flew by a monstrous crow,
As big as a tar barrel,
Which frightened both the heroes so,
They quite forgot their quarrel.

## OH, DEAR!

Dear, dear! what can the matter be?
Two old women got up in an apple-
    tree;
One came down, and the other
    stayed till Saturday.

## OLD MOTHER GOOSE

Old Mother Goose, when
    She wanted to wander,
Would ride through the air
    On a very fine gander.

## LITTLE JUMPING JOAN

Here am I, little jumping Joan,
When nobody's with me
    I'm always alone.

## PAT-A-CAKE

Pat-a-cake, pat-a-cake,
    Baker's man!
So I do, master,
    As fast as I can.

Pat it, and prick it,
    And mark it with T,
Put it in the oven
    For Tommy and me.

## MONEY AND THE MARE

"Lend me thy mare to ride a mile.
"She is lamed, leaping over a stile.

"Alack! and I must keep the fair!
I'll give thee money for thy mare."

"Oh, oh! say you so?
Money will make the mare to go!

## ROBIN REDBREAST

Little Robin Redbreast sat upon a tree
Up went Pussy-Cat, down went he,
Down came Pussy-Cat, away Robi
    ran,
Says little Robin Redbreast: "Catc
    me if you can!"

Little Robin Redbreast jumped upo
    a spade,
Pussy-Cat jumped after him, an
    then he was afraid.
Little Robin chirped and sang, an
    what did Pussy say?
Pussy-Cat said: "Mew, mew, mew,
    and Robin flew away.

PAT-A-CAKE

## A MELANCHOLY SONG

Trip upon trenchers,
And dance upon dishes,
My mother sent me for some barm,
    some barm;
She bid me go lightly,
And come again quickly,
For fear the young men should do
    me some harm.
Yet did n't you see, yet did n't you
    see,
What naughty tricks they put upon
    me?

They broke my
    pitcher
And spilt the
    water,
And huffed my
    mother,
And chid her
    daughter,
And kissed my
    sister instead
    of me.

## JACK

Jack be nimble, Jack be
    quick,
Jack jump over the candle-
    stick.

## GOING TO ST. IVES

As I was going to St. Ives
I met a man with seven wives.
Every wife had seven sacks,
Every sack had seven cats,
Every cat had seven kits.
Kits, cats, sacks, and wives,
How many were going to St. Ive

16

## BEES

A swarm of bees in May
Is worth a load of hay;
A swarm of bees in June
Is worth a silver spoon;
A swarm of bees in July
Is not worth a fly.

## COME OUT TO PLAY

Girls and boys, come out to play,
The moon doth shine as bright as
    day;
Leave your supper, and leave your
    sleep,
And come with your playfellows
    into the street.
Come with a whoop, come with a
    call,
Come with a good will or not at all.
Up the ladder and down the wall,
A half-penny roll will serve us all.
You find milk, and I'll find flour,
And we'll have a pudding in half
    an hour.

## THIRTY DAYS HATH
## SEPTEMBER

Thirty days hath September,
April, June, and November;
February has twenty-eight alone,
All the rest have thirty-one,
Excepting leap-year, that's the time
When February's days are twenty-
    nine.

## BABY DOLLY

Hush, baby, my dolly, I pray you
    don't cry,
And I'll give you some bread, and
    some milk by-and-by;
Or perhaps you like custard, or,
    maybe, a tart,
Then to either you're welcome, with
    all my heart.

TO MARKET, TO MARKET, TO BUY A FAT PIG

## IF WISHES WERE HORSES

If wishes were horses, beggars would
ride.

If turnips were watches, I would
wear one by my side.
And if "ifs" and "ands"
Were pots and pans,
There'd be no work for tinkers!

## TO MARKET

To market, to market, to buy a fat
pig,

Home again, home again, jiggety jig.

To market, to market, to buy a fat
hog,

Home again, home again, jiggety
jog.

To market, to market, to buy a plum
bun,

Home again, home again, market is
done.

## OLD CHAIRS TO MEND

If I'd as much money as I could
spend,

I never would cry old chairs to
mend;

Old chairs to mend, old chairs to
mend;

I never would cry old chairs to mend.

If I'd as much money as I could
tell,

I never would cry old clothes to
sell;

Old clothes to sell, old clothes to
sell;

I never would cry old clothes to sell.

## ROBIN AND RICHARD

Robin and Richard were two pretty men,
They lay in bed till the clock struck ten;
Then up starts Robin and looks at the sky,
"Oh, brother Richard, the sun's very high!
You go before, with the bottle and bag,
And I will come after on little Jack Nag."

## A MAN AND A MAID

There was a little man,
Who wooed a little maid,
And he said, "Little maid, will you
wed, wed, wed?
I have little more to say,
So will you, yea or nay,
For least said is soonest mended-ded,
ded, ded."

The little maid replied,
"Should I be your little bride,
Pray what must we have for to eat,
eat, eat?
Will the flame that you're so
rich in
Light a fire in the kitchen?
Or the little god of love turn the
spit, spit, spit?"

## HERE GOES MY LORD

Here goes my lord
A trot, a trot, a trot, a trot,
Here goes my lady
A canter, a canter, a canter, a canter!

Here goes my young master
Jockey-hitch, jockey-hitch, jockey-
hitch, jockey-hitch!
Here goes my young miss
An amble, an amble, an amble, an
amble!

The footman lags behind to tipple
ale and wine,
And goes gallop, a gallop, a gallop,
to make up his time.

## THE CLEVER HEN

I had a little hen, the prettiest
ever seen,
She washed me the dishes and
kept the house clean;
She went to the mill to fetch me
some flour,
She brought it home in less than
an hour;
She baked me my bread, she
brewed me my ale,
She sat by the fire and told
many a fine tale.

LUCY LOCKET

## TWO BIRDS

There were two birds sat on a stone,
    Fa, la, la, la, lal, de;
One flew away, and then there was
    one,
    Fa, la, la, la, lal, de;
The other bird flew after,
And then there was none,
    Fa, la, la, la, lal, de;
And so the stone
Was left alone,
    Fa, la, la, la, lal, de.

## LEG OVER LEG

Leg over leg,
As the dog went to Dover;
When he came to a stile,
Jump, he went over.

## LUCY LOCKET

Lucy Locket lost her pocket,
Kitty Fisher found it;
Nothing in it, nothing in it,
But the binding round it.

## WHEN JENNY WREN WAS YOUNG

'Twas once upon a time, when
    Jenny Wren was young,
So daintily she danced and so pret-
    tily she sung,
Robin Redbreast lost his heart, for
    he was a gallant bird.
So he doffed his hat to Jenny Wren,
    requesting to be heard.

"Oh, dearest Jenny Wren, if you
    will but be mine,
You shall feed on cherry pie and
    drink new currant wine,
I'll dress you like a goldfinch or any
    peacock gay,
So, dearest Jen, if you'll be mine, let
    us appoint the day."

Jenny blushed behind her fan and
    thus declared her mind:
"Since, dearest Bob, I love you well,
    I'll take your offer kind.
Cherry pie is very nice and so is
    currant wine,
But I must wear my plain brown
    gown and never go too fine."

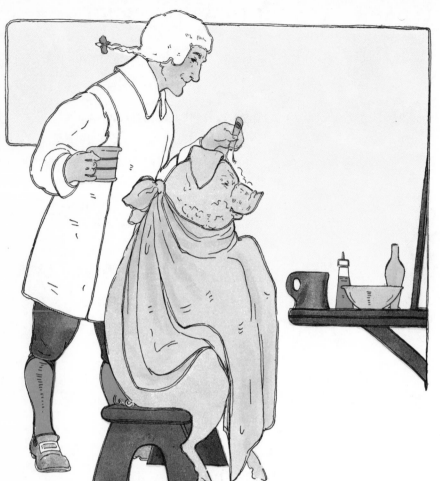

# SOLOMON GRUNDY

Solomon Grundy,
Born on a Monday,
Christened on Tuesday,
Married on Wednesday,
Took ill on Thursday,
Worse on Friday,
Died on Saturday,
Buried on Sunday.
This is the end
Of Solomon Grundy.

## BARBER

Barber, barber, shave a pig.
How many hairs will make a wig?
Four and twenty; that's enough.
Give the barber a pinch of snuff.

## THE FLYING PIG

Dickory, dickory, dare,
The pig flew up in the air;
The man in brown soon brought
    him down,
        Dickory,
            dickory,
                dare.

## HUSH-A-BYE

Hush-a-bye, baby, on the tree top!
When the wind blows the cradle
 will rock;
When the bough breaks the cradle
 will fall;
Down will come baby, bough, cradle
 and all.

## BURNIE BEE

Burnie bee, burnie bee,
Tell me when your wedding be?
If it be to-morrow day,
Take your wings and fly away.

## THREE WISE MEN OF GOTHAM

Three wise men of Gotham
Went to sea in a bowl;
If the bowl had been stronger
My song had been longer.

## THE HUNTER OF REIGATE

A man went a-hunting at Reigate,
And wished to leap over a high
 gate.
Says the owner, "Go round,
With your gun and your hound,
For you never shall leap over my
 gate."

## PIPPEN HILL

As I was going up Pippen Hill,
    Pippen Hill was dirty;
There I met a pretty Miss,
    And she dropped me a
        curtsy.

Little Miss, pretty Miss,
    Blessings light upon you;
If I had half-a-crown a day,
    I'd spend it all upon you.

## LITTLE POLLY FLINDERS

Little Polly Flinders
Sat among the cinders
    Warming her pretty little toes;
Her mother came and caught her,
Whipped her little daughter
    For spoiling her nice new
        clothes.

## RIDE AWAY, RIDE AWAY

Ride away, ride away,
    Johnny shall ride,
And he shall have pussy-cat
    Tied to one side;
And he shall have little dog
    Tied to the other,
And Johnny shall ride
    To see his grandmother.

## PUSSY-CAT AND QUEEN

"Pussy-cat, pussy-cat,
    Where have you been?"
"I've been to London
    To look at the Queen."

"Pussy-cat, pussy-cat,
    What did you there?"
"I frightened a little mouse
    Under the chair."

## THE WINDS

Mister East gave a feast;
Mister North laid the cloth;
Mister West did his best;
Mister South burnt his mouth
Eating cold potato.

PUSSY-CAT AND QUEEN

## CLAP HANDIES

Clap, clap handies,

Mammie's wee, wee ain;

Clap, clap handies,

Daddie's comin' hame,

Hame till his bonny wee bit laddie;

Clap, clap handies,

My wee, wee ain.

## CHRISTMAS

Christmas comes but once a year,

And when it comes it brings good

cheer.

## ELIZABETH

Elizabeth, Elspeth, Betsy, and
Bess,

They all went together to seek a
bird's nest;

They found a bird's nest with five
eggs in,

They all took one, and left four in.

## JUST LIKE ME

"I went up one pair of stairs."
"Just like me."

"I went up two pairs of stairs."
"Just like me."

"I went into a room."
"Just like me."

"I looked out of a window."
"Just like me."

"And there I saw a monkey."
"Just like me."

## PLAY DAYS

How many days has my baby to
play?

Saturday, Sunday, Monday,

Tuesday, Wednesday, Thursday,
Friday,

Saturday, Sunday, Monday.

# HEIGH-HO, THE CARRION CROW

A carrion crow sat on an oak,
  Fol de riddle, lol de riddle,
    hi ding do,
Watching a tailor shape his
    cloak;
  Sing heigh-ho, the carrion
    crow,
  Fol de riddle, lol de riddle,
    hi ding do!

Wife, bring me my old bent bow,
  Fol de riddle, lol de riddle,
    hi ding do,
That I may shoot yon carrion
    crow;
  Sing heigh-ho, the carrion
    crow,
  Fol de riddle, lol de riddle,
    hi ding do!

The tailor he shot, and missed
    his mark,
  Fol de riddle, lol de riddle,
    hi ding do!
And shot his own sow quite
    through the heart;
  Sing heigh-ho, the carrion crow,
  Fol de riddle, lol de riddle,
    hi ding do!

Wife! bring brandy in a spoon,
  Fol de riddle, lol de riddle,
    hi ding do!
For our old sow is in a swoon;
  Sing heigh-ho, the carrion
    crow,
  Fol de riddle, lol de riddle,
    hi ding do!

29

## A B C

Great A, little a,
Bouncing B!
The cat's in the cupboard,
And can't see me.

## A NEEDLE AND THREAD

Old Mother Twitchett had but
one eye,
And a long tail which she let fly;
And every time she went through
a gap,
A bit of her tail she left in a trap.

## BANBURY CROSS

Ride a cock-horse to Banbury Cross,
To see an old lady upon a white
horse.
Rings on her fingers, and bells on
her toes,
She shall have music wherever she
goes.

## THE MAN IN OUR TOWN

There was a man in our town,
        And he was wondrous wise,
He jumped into a bramble bush,
        And scratched out both his
        eyes;
But when he saw his eyes were out,
        With all his might and main,
He jumped into another bush,
        And scratched 'em in again.

RIDE A COCK-HORSE TO BANBURY CROSS

## GEORGY PORGY

Georgy Porgy, pudding and pie,
Kissed the girls and made them cry.
When the boys came out to play,
Georgy Porgy ran away.

## FOR EVERY EVIL

For every evil under the sun
There is a remedy or there is none.
If there be one, seek till you find it;
If there be none, never mind it.

## CUSHY COW

Cushy cow, bonny, let down thy milk,
And I will give thee a gown of silk;
A gown of silk and a silver tee,
If thou wilt let down thy milk to me.

## WEE WILLIE WINKIE

Wee Willie Winkie runs through
    the town,
Upstairs and downstairs, in his
    nightgown;
Rapping at the window, crying
    through the lock,
"Are the children in their beds?
    Now it's eight o'clock."

## ABOUT THE BUSH

About the bush, Willie,
    About the beehive,
About the bush, Willie,
    I'll meet thee alive.

## SEE-SAW

See-saw, Margery Daw,
Sold her bed and lay upon straw.

## ROBIN-A-BOBBIN

Robin-a-Bobbin
Bent his bow,
Shot at a pigeon,
And killed a crow.

## JOHN SMITH

Is John Smith within?
Yes, that he is.
Can he set a shoe?
Ay, marry, two.
Here a nail, there a nail,
Tick, tack, too.

THREE BLIND MICE

## SIMPLE SIMON

Simple Simon met a pieman,
    Going to the fair;
Says Simple Simon to the pieman,
    "Let me taste your ware."

Says the pieman to Simple Simon,
    "Show me first your penny,"
Says Simple Simon to the pieman,
    "Indeed, I have not any."

Simple Simon went a-fishing
    For to catch a whale;
All the water he could find
    Was in his mother's pail!

Simple Simon went to look
    If plums grew on a thistle;
He pricked his fingers very much,
    Which made poor Simon
      whistle.

He went to catch a dicky bird,
    And thought he could not fail,
Because he had a little salt,
    To put upon its tail.

He went for water with a sieve,
    But soon it ran all through;
And now poor Simple Simon
    Bids you all adieu.

## THREE BLIND MICE

Three blind mice! See how they run!
They all ran after the farmer's wife,
Who cut off their tails with a carv-
    ing knife.
Did you ever see such a thing in
    your life
As three blind mice?

## FIVE TOES

This little pig went to market;
This little pig stayed at home;
This little pig had roast beef;
This little pig had none;
This little pig said, "Wee, wee!
I can't find my way home."

The drake was a-swimming with
his curly tail;
The little man made it his mark,
mark, mark.
He let off his gun, but he fired
too soon,
And the drake flew away with a
quack, quack, quack.

## DOCTOR FOSTER

Doctor Foster went to Glo'ster,
In a shower of rain;
He stepped in a puddle, up to his
middle,
And never went there again.

## A LITTLE MAN

There was a little man, and he had
a little gun,
And his bullets were made of
lead, lead, lead;
He went to the brook, and saw a
little duck,
And shot it right through the
head, head, head.

He carried it home to his old wife
Joan,
And bade her a fire to make,
make, make.
To roast the little duck he had shot
in the brook,
And he'd go and fetch the drake,
drake, drake.

## DIDDLE DIDDLE DUMPLING

Diddle diddle dumpling, my son John
Went to bed with his breeches on,
One stocking off, and one stocking on;
Diddle diddle dumpling, my son John.

## JERRY HALL

Jerry Hall, he was so small,
A rat could eat him, hat and all.

## LENGTHENING DAYS

As the days grow longer
The storms grow stronger.

CURLY-LOCKS, CURLY-LOCKS, WILT THOU BE MINE?

## THE BLACK HEN

Hickety, pickety, my black hen,
She lays eggs for gentlemen;
Gentlemen come every day
To see what my black hen
    doth lay.

## THE MIST

A hill full, a hole full,
Yet you cannot catch a bowl full.

## A CANDLE

Little Nanny Etticoat
In a white petticoat,
And a red nose;
The longer she stands
The shorter she grows.

## MISS MUFFET

Little Miss Muffet
Sat on a tuffet,
Eating of curds and whey;
    There came a big spider,
    And sat down beside her,
And frightened Miss Muffet away.

## CURLY-LOCKS

Curly-locks, Curly-locks, wilt thou be mine?
Thou shalt not wash the dishes, nor yet feed
    the swine;
But sit on a cushion, and sew a fine seam,
And feed upon strawberries, sugar, and
    cream.

## HUMPTY DUMPTY

Humpty Dumpty sat on a wall,
Humpty Dumpty had a great fall;
All the King's horses, and all the
 King's men
Cannot put Humpty Dumpty together
 again.

## ONE, TWO, THREE

One, two, three, four, five,
Once I caught a fish alive.
Six, seven, eight, nine, ten,
But I let it go again.
Why did you let it go?
Because it bit my finger so.
Which finger did it bite?
The little one upon the right.

## THE DOVE AND THE WREN

The dove says coo, coo, what shall
　I do?
I can scarce maintain two.
Pooh, pooh! says the wren, I've got
　ten,
And keep them all like gentlemen.

## MASTER I HAVE

Master I have, and I am his man,
　Gallop a dreary dun;
Master I have, and I am his man,
　And I'll get a wife as fast as
　　I can;
With a heighty gaily gamberally,
　Higgledy piggledy, niggledy,
　　niggledy,
　Gallop a dreary dun.

## PINS

See a pin and pick it up,
All the day you'll have good luck.
See a pin and let it lay,
Bad luck you'll have all the day.

## SHALL WE GO A-SHEARING?

"Old woman, old woman, shall we
　go a-shearing?"
"Speak a little louder, sir, I am
　very thick of hearing."
"Old woman, old woman, shall I
　kiss you dearly?"
"Thank you, kind sir, I hear you
　very clearly."

GOOSEY, GOOSEY, GANDER

# GOOSEY, GOOSEY, GANDER

Goosey, goosey, gander,
  Whither dost thou wander?
Upstairs and downstairs
  And in my lady's chamber.

There I met an old man
  Who would n't say his prayers;
I took him by the left leg,
  And threw him down the stairs.

# OLD MOTHER HUBBARD

Old Mother Hubbard
Went to the cupboard,
  To give her poor dog a bone;
But when she got there
The cupboard was bare,
  And so the poor dog had none.

She went to the baker's
  To buy him some bread;
When she came back
  The dog was dead.

She went to the undertaker's
  To buy him a coffin;
When she got back
  The dog was laughing.

She took a clean dish
  To get him some tripe;
When she came back
  He was smoking a pipe.

She went to the alehouse
  To get him some beer;
When she came back
  The dog sat in a chair.

She went to the tavern
  For white wine and red;
When she came back
  The dog stood on his head.

She went to the hatter's
  To buy him a hat;
When she came back
  He was feeding the cat.

She went to the barber's
  To buy him a wig;
When she came back
  He was dancing a jig.

She went to the fruiterer's
  To buy him some fruit;
When she came back
  He was playing the flute.

She went to the tailor's
  To buy him a coat;
When she came back
  He was riding a goat.

She went to the cobbler's
  To buy him some shoes;
When she came back
  He was reading the news.

She went to the sempster's
  To buy him some linen;
When she came back
  The dog was a-spinning.

She went to the hosier's
  To buy him some hose;
When she came back
  He was dressed in his clothes.

The dame made a curtsy,
  The dog made a bow;
The dame said, "Your servant,"
  The dog said, "Bow-wow."

## THE COCK AND THE HEN

  "Cock, cock, cock, cock,
  I've laid an egg,
  Am I to gang ba—are-foot?"

  "Hen, hen, hen, hen,
  I've been up and down
  To every shop in town,
  And cannot find a shoe
  To fit your foot,
  If I'd crow my hea—art out."

## BLUE BELL BOY

I had a little boy,
  And called him Blue Bell;
Gave him a little work,—
  He did it very well.

I bade him go upstairs
  To bring me a gold pin;
In coal scuttle fell he,
  Up to his little chin.

He went to the garden
  To pick a little sage;
He tumbled on his nose,
  And fell into a rage.

He went to the cellar
  To draw a little beer;
And quickly did return
  To say there was none there.

## WHY MAY NOT I LOVE JOHNNY?

Johnny shall have a new bonnet,
   And Johnny shall go to the fair,
And Johnny shall have a blue ribbon
   To tie up his bonny brown hair.

And why may not I love Johnny?
   And why may not Johnny
      love me?
And why may not I love Johnny
   As well as another body?

And here's a leg for a stocking,
   And here's a foot for a shoe,
And he has a kiss for his daddy,
   And two for his mammy, I trow.

And why may not I love Johnny?
   And why may not Johnny love
      me?
And why may not I love Johnny
   As well as another body?

## JACK JELF

Little Jack Jelf
Was put on the shelf
Because he could not spell "pie";
   When his aunt, Mrs. Grace,
   Saw his sorrowful face,
She could not help saying, "Oh, fie!"

And since Master Jelf
Was put on the shelf
Because he could not spell "pie,"
   Let him stand there so grim,
   And no more about him,
For I wish him a very good-bye!

JACK SPRAT

## JACK SPRAT

Jack Sprat
Could eat no fat,
His wife could eat no lean;
And so,
Betwixt them both,
They licked the platter clean.

## HUSH-A-BYE

Hush-a-bye, baby,
Daddy is near;
Mamma is a lady,
And that's very clear.

## DAFFODILS

Daffy-down-dilly has come to town
In a yellow petticoat and a green
gown.

## THE GIRL IN THE LANE

The girl in the lane, that couldn't
speak plain,
Cried, "Gobble, gobble, gobble":
The man on the hill that couldn't
stand still,
Went hobble hobble, hobble.

## HUSH-A-BYE

Hush-a-bye, baby, lie still with thy
daddy,
Thy mammy has gone to the
mill,
To get some meal to bake a cake,
So pray, my dear baby, lie still.

## NANCY DAWSON

Nancy Dawson was so fine
She wouldn't get up to serve the
swine;
She lies in bed till eight or
nine,
So it's Oh, poor Nancy Dawson.

And do ye ken Nancy Dawson
honey?
The wife who sells the barley, honey
She won't get up to feed her swine,
And do ye ken Nancy Dawson
honey?

## HANDY PANDY

Handy Pandy, Jack-a-dandy,
Loves plum cake and sugar candy.
He bought some at a grocer's shop,
And out he came, hop, hop, hop!

## JACK AND JILL

Jack and Jill went up the hill,
　To fetch a pail of water;
Jack fell down, and broke his crown,
　And Jill came tumbling after.

Then up Jack got and off did trot,
　As fast as he could caper,
To old Dame Dob, who patched his
　　nob
　With vinegar and brown paper.

## THE ALPHABET

A, B, C, and D,
Pray, playmates, agree.
E, F, and G,
Well, so it shall be.
J, K, and L,
In peace we will dwell.
M, N, and O,
To play let us go.
P, Q, R, and S,
Love may we possess.
W, X, and Y,
Will not quarrel or die.
Z, and ampersand,
Go to school at command.

## DANCE TO YOUR DADDIE

Dance to your daddie,
My bonnie laddie;
Dance to your daddie, my bonnie
    lamb;
You shall get a fishy,
On a little dishy;
You shall get a fishy, when the boat
    comes home.

## ONE MISTY MOISTY
## MORNING

One misty moisty morning,
    When cloudy was the weather,
I chanced to meet an old man,
    Clothed all in leather.
He began to compliment
    And I began to grin.
How do you do? And how do you do?
    And how do you do again?

## ROBIN HOOD AND
## LITTLE JOHN

Robin Hood, Robin Hood,
    Is in the mickle wood!
Little John, Little John,
    He to the town is gone.

Robin Hood, Robin Hood,
    Telling his beads,
All in the greenwood
    Among the green weeds.

Little John, Little John,
    If he comes no more,
Robin Hood, Robin Hood,
    We shall fret full sore!

## RAIN

Rain, rain, go to Spain,
And never come back again.

ROBIN HOOD

## THE ROBINS

A robin and a robin's son
Once went to town to buy a bun.
They couldn't decide on plum or
    plain,
And so they went back home again.

## THE OLD MAN

There was an old man
In a velvet coat,
He kissed a maid
And gave her a groat.
The groat it was crack'd
And would not go,—
Ah, old man, do you serve me so?

## THE OLD WOMAN FROM FRANCE

There came an old woman from
    France
Who taught grown-up children to
    dance;
  But they were so stiff,
  She sent them home in a sniff,
This sprightly old woman from
    France.

## TEETH AND GUMS

Thirty white horses upon a red hill,
Now they tramp, now they champ,
    now they stand still.

## IF ALL THE SEAS WERE ONE SEA

If all the seas were one sea,
What a *great* sea that would be!
And if all the trees were one tree,
What a *great* tree that would be!
And if all the axes were one axe,
What a *great* axe that would be!
And if all the men were one man,
What a *great* man he would be!
And if the *great* man took the *great*
    axe,
And cut down the *great* tree,
And let it fall into the *great* sea,
What a splish splash *that* would be!

## T'OTHER LITTLE TUNE

I won't be my father's Jack,
  I won't be my father's Jill;
I will be the fiddler's wife,
  And have music when I will.
    T'other little tune,
    T'other little tune,
    Prithee, Love, play me
    T'other little tune.

## MY KITTEN

Hey, my kitten, my kitten,
  And hey, my kitten, my deary!
Such a sweet pet as this
  Was neither far nor neary.

HERE SITS THE LORD MAYOR

HERE SITS THE LORD MAYOR

## FOREHEAD, EYES, CHEEKS, NOSE, MOUTH, AND CHIN

Here sits the Lord Mayor,
　　Here sit his two men,
Here sits the cock,
　　Here sits the hen,
Here sit the little chickens,
　　Here they run in.
Chin-chopper, chin-chopper, chin
　　chopper, chin!

## TWO PIGEONS

I had two pigeons bright and gay,
They flew from me the other day.
What was the reason they did go?
I cannot tell, for I do not know.

## PANCAKE DAY

Great A, little a,
This is pancake day;
Toss the ball high,
Throw the ball low,
Those that come after
May sing heigh-ho!

## A PLUM PUDDING

Flour of England, fruit of Spain,
　　Met together in a shower of rain;
Put in a bag tied round with a
　　string;
If you'll tell me this riddle,
I'll give you a ring.

## A SURE TEST

If you are to be a gentleman,
    As I suppose you'll be,
You'll neither laugh nor smile,
    For a tickling of the knee.

## LOCK AND KEY

"I am a gold lock."
"I am a gold key."
"I am a silver lock."
"I am a silver key."
"I am a brass lock."
"I am a brass key."
"I am a lead lock."
"I am a lead key."
"I am a don lock."
"I am a don key!"

## THE LION AND THE UNICORN

The Lion and the Unicorn were
    fighting for the crown,
The Lion beat the Unicorn all
    around the town.
Some gave them white bread, and
    some gave them brown,
Some gave them plum-cake, and
    sent them out of town.

## THE MERCHANTS OF LONDON

Hey diddle dinkety poppety pet,
The merchants of London they wear
    scarlet,
Silk in the collar and gold in the
    hem,
So merrily march the merchant
    men.

## I'LL TELL YOU A STORY

I'll tell you a story
About Jack-a-Nory:
And now my story's begun.
I'll tell you another
About his brother:
And now my story is done.

## A STRANGE OLD WOMAN

There was an old woman, and what
do you think?
She lived upon nothing but victuals
and drink;
Victuals and drink were the chief
of her diet,
And yet this old woman could
never be quiet.

## I HAD A LITTLE HUSBAND

I had a little husband no bigger
than my thumb,
I put him in a pint pot, and there
I bid him drum,
I bought a little handkerchief to
wipe his little nose,
And a pair of little garters to tie his
little hose.

## TO BABYLON

How many miles is it to Babylon?—
Threescore miles and ten.
Can I get there by candle-light?—
Yes, and back again.
If your heels are nimble and light,
You may get there by candle-light.

## BAA, BAA, BLACK SHEEP

Baa, baa, black sheep,
Have you any wool?
Yes, marry, have I,
Three bags full;

One for my master,
One for my dame,
But none for the little boy
Who cries in the lane.

## LITTLE FRED

When little Fred went to bed,
  He always said his prayers;
He kissed mamma, and then papa,
  And straightway went upstairs.

## SLEEP, BABY, SLEEP

Sleep, baby, sleep,
Our cottage vale is deep:
The little lamb is on the green,
With woolly fleece so soft and clean—
Sleep, baby, sleep.

Sleep, baby, sleep,
Down where the woodbines creep;
Be always like the lamb so mild,
A kind, and sweet, and gentle child.
Sleep, baby, sleep.

## CRY, BABY

Cry, baby, cry,
Put your finger in your eye,
And tell your mother it wasn't I.

BAA, BAA, BLACK SHEEP

# THE CAT AND THE FIDDLE

Hey, diddle, diddle!
The cat and the fiddle,
The cow jumped over the moon;
The little dog laughed
To see such sport,
And the dish ran away with the spoon.

## DOCTOR FELL

I do not like thee, Doctor Fell;
The reason why I cannot tell;
But this I know, and know full well,
I do not like thee, Doctor Fell!

## A COUNTING-OUT RHYME

Hickery, dickery, 6 and 7,
Alabone, Crackabone, 10 and 11,
Spin, spun, muskidun,
Twiddle 'em, twaddle 'em, 21.

# JACK AND HIS FIDDLE

"Jacky, come and give me thy fiddle,
    If ever thou mean to thrive."
"Nay, I'll not give my fiddle
    To any man alive.

"If I should give my fiddle,
    They'll think that I've gone mad;
For many a joyous day
    My fiddle and I have had."

## BUTTONS

Buttons, a farthing a pair!
Come, who will buy them of me?
They're round and sound and pretty,
And fit for girls of the city.
Come, who will buy them of me?
Buttons, a farthing a pair!

## HOT BOILED BEANS

Ladies and gentlemen come to
    supper—
Hot boiled beans and very good
    butter.

When the pie was opened
  The birds began to sing;
Was not that a dainty dish
  To set before the king?

The king was in his counting-house,
  Counting out his money;
The queen was in the parlor,
  Eating bread and honey.

The maid was in the garden,
  Hanging out the clothes;
When down came a blackbird
  And snapped off her nose.

## LITTLE PUSSY

I like little Pussy,
  Her coat is so warm,
And if I don't hurt her
  She'll do me no harm;
So I'll not pull her tail,
  Nor drive her away,
But Pussy and I
  Very gently will play.

## SING A SONG OF SIXPENCE

Sing a song of sixpence,
  A pocket full of rye;
Four-and-twenty blackbirds
  Baked in a pie!

SING A SONG OF SIXPENCE

## TOMMY TITTLEMOUSE

Little Tommy Tittlemouse
Lived in a little house;
He caught fishes
In other men's ditches.

## THE DERBY RAM

As I was going to Derby all on a
market-day,
I met the finest ram, sir, that ever
was fed upon hay;
Upon hay, upon hay, upon hay;
I met the finest ram, sir, that ever
was fed upon hay.
This ram was fat behind, sir; this
ram was fat before;
This ram was ten yards round, sir;
indeed, he was no more;
No more, no more, no more;
This ram was ten yards round, sir;
indeed, he was no more.

The horns that grew on his head, sir,
they were so wondrous high,
As I've been plainly told, sir, they
reached up to the sky.
The sky, the sky, the sky;
As I've been plainly told, sir, they
reached up to the sky.

The tail that grew from his back, sir,
was six yards and an ell;
And it was sent to Derby to toll the
market bell;
The bell, the bell, the bell;
And it was sent to Derby to toll
the market bell.

This is the way we wash our clothes,
On a cold and frosty morning.

This is the way we go to school,
Go to school, go to school,
This is the way we go to school,
On a cold and frosty morning.

This is the way we come out of school,
Come out of school, come out of
    school,
This is the way we come out of
    school,
On a cold and frosty morning.

## THE HOBBY-HORSE

I had a little hobby-horse,
    And it was dapple gray;
Its head was made of pea-straw,
    Its tail was made of hay.

I sold it to an old woman
    For a copper groat;
And I'll not sing my song again
    Without another coat.

## THE MULBERRY BUSH

Here we go round the mulberry bush,
The mulberry bush, the mulberry
    bush,
Here we go round the mulberry bush.
On a cold and frosty morning.

This is the way we wash our hands,
Wash our hands, wash our hands,
This is the way we wash our hands,
On a cold and frosty morning.

This is the way we wash our clothes.
Wash our clothes, wash our clothes,

## YOUNG LAMBS TO SELL

If I'd as much money as I could tell,
I never would cry young lambs to sell;
Young lambs to sell, young lambs to sell;
I never would cry young lambs to sell.

## OLD WOMAN, OLD WOMAN

There was an old woman tossed in
    a basket,
    Seventeen times as high as the
      moon;
But where she was going no mortal
    could tell,
    For under her arm she carried a
      broom.
"Old woman, old woman, old
    woman," said I,
    "Whither, oh whither, oh whither
      so high?"
"To sweep the cobwebs from the sky;
    And I'll be with you by-and-by."

## THE FIRST OF MAY

The fair maid who, the first of May,
Goes to the fields at break of day,
And washes in dew from the haw-
    thorn-tree,
Will ever after handsome be.

## BOY AND THE SPARROW

A little cock-sparrow sat on a green
    tree,
And he chirruped, he chirruped, so
    merry was he;
A naughty boy came with his wee
    bow and arrow,
Determined to shoot this little cock-
    sparrow.
"This little cock-sparrow shall make
    me a stew,
And his giblets shall make me a
    little pie, too."
"Oh, no," says the sparrow "I won't
    make a stew."
So he flapped his wings and away
    he flew.

THE OLD WOMAN TOSSED IN A BASKET

## SULKY SUE

Here's Sulky Sue,
What shall we do?
Turn her face to the wall
Till she comes to.


## THE HOUSE THAT JACK BUILT

This is the house that Jack built.
This is the malt
That lay in the house that Jack
 built.

This is the rat,
That ate the malt
That lay in the house that Jack
 built.

This is the cat,
That killed the rat,

That ate the malt
That lay in the house that Jack
 built.

This is the dog,
That worried the cat,
That killed the rat,
That ate the malt
That lay in the house that Jack
 built.

This is the cow with the crumpled
 horn,
That tossed the dog,
That worried the cat,
That killed the rat,
That ate the malt
That lay in the house that Jack
 built.

This is the maiden all forlorn,
That milked the cow with the
 crumpled horn,
That tossed the dog,
That worried the cat,
That killed the rat,
That ate the malt
That lay in the house that Jack
 built.

This is the man all tattered and
 torn,
That kissed the maiden all forlorn,
That milked the cow with the
 crumpled horn,
That tossed the dog,
That worried the cat,
That killed the rat,

That ate the malt

That lay in the house that Jack built.

This is the priest all shaven and shorn,

That married the man all tattered and torn,

That kissed the maiden all forlorn,

That milked the cow with the crumpled horn,

That tossed the dog,

That worried the cat,

That killed the rat,

That ate the malt

That lay in the house that Jack built.

This is the cock that crowed in the morn,

That waked the priest all shaven and shorn,

That married the man all tattered and torn,

That kissed the maiden all forlorn,

That milked the cow with the crumpled horn,

That tossed the dog,

That worried the cat,

That killed the rat,

That ate the malt

That lay in the house that Jack built.

This is the farmer sowing the corn,

That kept the cock that crowed in the morn.

That waked the priest all shaven and shorn,

That married the man all tattered and torn,

That kissed the maiden all forlorn,

That milked the cow with the crumpled horn,

That tossed the dog,

That worried the cat,

That killed the rat,

That ate the malt

That lay in the house that Jack built.

## SATURDAY, SUNDAY

On Saturday night
    Shall be all my care
To powder my locks
    And curl my hair.

On Sunday morning
    My love will come in,
When he will marry me
    With a gold ring.

THE OLD WOMAN AND THE PEDLAR

# LITTLE JENNY WREN

Little Jenny Wren fell sick,
    Upon a time;
In came Robin Redbreast
    And brought her cake and
    wine.

"Eat well of my cake, Jenny,
    Drink well of my wine."
"Thank you, Robin, kindly,
    You shall be mine."

Jenny she got well,
    And stood upon her feet,
And told Robin plainly
    She loved him not a bit.

Robin being angry,
    Hopped upon a twig,
Saying, "Out upon you!  Fie upon
    you!
    Bold-faced jig!"

# THE OLD WOMAN AND
# THE PEDLAR

There was an old woman, as I've
    heard tell,
She went to market her eggs for to
    sell;
She went to market all on a market-
    day,
And she fell asleep on the King's
    highway.

There came by a pedlar whose
    name was Stout,
He cut her petticoats all round
    about;
He cut her petticoats up to the
    knees,
Which made the old woman to shiver
    and freeze.

When the little old woman first did
    wake,
She began to shiver and she began
    to shake;
She began to wonder and she began
    to cry,
"Lauk a mercy on me, this can't
    be I!

"But if it be I, as I hope it be,
I've a little dog at home, and he'll
    know me;
If it be I, he'll wag his little tail,
And if it be not I, he'll loudly bark
    and wail."

Home went the little woman all in
    the dark;
Up got the little dog, and he began
    to bark;
He began to bark, so she began to
    cry,
"Lauk a mercy on me, this is none
    of I!"

## BOBBY SNOOKS

Little Bobby Snooks was fond of
    his books,
    And loved by his usher and mas-
        ter;
But naughty Jack Spry, he got a
    black eye,
    And carries his nose in a plaster.

## THE LITTLE MOPPET

    I had a little moppet,
    I put it in my pocket,
And fed it with corn and hay.
    There came a proud beggar.
    And swore he should have her;
And stole my little moppet away.

# I SAW A SHIP A-SAILING

I saw a ship a-sailing,
A-sailing on the sea;
And, oh! it was all laden
With pretty things for thee!

There were comfits in the cabin,
And apples in the hold;
The sails were made of silk,
And the masts were made of gold.

The four-and-twenty sailors
That stood between the decks,
Were four-and-twenty white mice
With chains about their necks.

The captain was a duck,
With a packet on his back;
And when the ship began to move,
The captain said, "Quack! Quack!"

## A WALNUT

As soft as silk, as white as milk,
As bitter as gall, a strong wall,
And a green coat covers me all.

## THE MAN IN THE MOON

The Man in the Moon came tumbling
   down,
   And asked the way to Norwich;
He went by the south, and burnt his
   mouth
   With eating cold pease porridge.

# ONE, HE LOVES

One, he loves; two, he loves;
Three, he loves, they say;
Four, he loves with all his heart;
Five, he casts away.
Six, he loves; seven, she loves;
Eight, they both love.
Nine, he comes; ten, he tarries;
Eleven, he courts; twelve, he mar-
   ries.

## BAT, BAT

Bat, bat,
Come under my hat,
And I'll give you a slice of bacon;
And when I bake
I'll give you a cake
If I am not mistaken.

HARK! HARK! THE DOGS DO BARK!

## MY LOVE

Saw ye aught of my love a-coming
from the market?
A peck of meal upon her back,
A babby in her basket;
Saw ye aught of my love a-coming
from the market?

## THE MAN OF BOMBAY

There was a fat man of Bombay,
Who was smoking one sunshiny day;
When a bird called a snipe
Flew away with his pipe,
Which vexed the fat man of Bombay

## HARK! HARK!

Hark, hark! the dogs do bark!
Beggars are coming to town:
Some in jags, and some in rags,
And some in velvet gown.

## THE HART

The hart he loves the high wood,
The hare she loves the hill;
The Knight he loves his bright
sword,
The Lady—loves her will.

## MY MAID MARY

My maid Mary she minds the dairy,
   While I go a-hoeing and mowing
      each morn;
Gaily run the reel and the little
      spinning wheel.
   While I am singing and mowing
      my corn.

## A DIFFICULT RHYME

What is the rhyme for porringer?
The king he had a daughter fair,
And gave the Prince of Orange her.

## POOR OLD ROBINSON CRUSOE!

Poor old Robinson Crusoe!
Poor old Robinson Crusoe!
   They made him a coat
   Of an old Nanny goat.
I wonder why they should do so!
   With a ring-a-ting-tang,
   And a ring-a-ting-tang,
Poor old Robinson Crusoe!

## A SIEVE

A riddle, a riddle, as I suppose,
A hundred eyes and never a nose!

## PRETTY JOHN WATTS

Pretty John Watts,
We are troubled with rats.
Will you drive them out of the
house?
We have mice, too, in plenty,
That feast in the pantry,
But let them stay
And nibble away,
What harm in a little brown mouse?

## GOOD ADVICE

Come when you're called,
Do what you're bid,
Shut the door after you,
And never be chid.

## I LOVE SIXPENCE

I love sixpence, a jolly, jolly
sixpence,
I love sixpence as my life;
I spent a penny of it, I spent a
penny of it,
I took a penny home to my
wife.

Oh, my little fourpence, a jolly,
jolly fourpence,
I love fourpence as my life;
I spent twopence of it, I spent twopence of it,
And I took twopence home to
my wife.

## BYE, BABY BUNTING

Bye, baby bunting,
Father's gone a-hunting,
Mother's gone a-milking,
Sister's gone a-silking,
And brother's gone to buy a skin
To wrap the baby bunting in.

## TOM, TOM, THE PIPER'S
SON

Tom, Tom, the piper's son,
Stole a pig, and away he run,
The pig was eat,
And Tom was beat,
And Tom ran crying down the
street.

## COMICAL FOLK

In a cottage in Fife
Lived a man and his wife
Who, believe me, were comical folk;
For, to people's surprise,
They both saw with their eyes,
And their tongues moved whenever
they spoke!

When they were asleep,
I'm told, that to keep
Their eyes open they could not
contrive;
They both walked on their feet,
And 'twas thought what they
eat
Helped, with drinking, to keep them
alive!

## COCK-CROW

Cocks crow in the morn
To tell us to rise,
And he who lies late
Will never be wise;
For early to bed
And early to rise,
Is the way to be healthy
And wealthy and wise.

## TOMMY SNOOKS

As Tommy Snooks and Bessy
Brooks
Were walking out one Sunday,
Says Tommy Snooks to Bessy
Brooks,
"Wilt marry me on Monday?"

COCK-CROW

## THE THREE SONS

There was an old woman had three
    sons,
Jerry and James and John,
Jerry was hanged, James was
    drowned,
John was lost and never was found;
And there was an end of her three
    sons,
Jerry and James and John!

## THE BLACKSMITH

"Robert Barnes, my fellow fine,
Can you shoe this horse of mine?"
"Yes, good sir, that I can,
As well as any other man;
There's a nail, and there's a prod,
Now, good sir, your horse is shod."

## TWO GRAY KITS

The two gray kits,
And the gray kits' mother,
    All went over
The bridge together.

The bridge broke down,
    They all fell in;
"May the rats go with you,"
    Says Tom Bolin.

## ONE, TWO, BUCKLE MY SHOE

One, two,
Buckle my shoe;
Three, four,
Knock at the door;
Five, six,
Pick up sticks;
Seven, eight,
Lay them straight;
Nine, ten,
A good, fat hen;
Eleven, twelve,
Dig and delve;
Thirteen, fourteen,
Maids a-courting;
Fifteen, sixteen,
Maids in the kitchen;
Seventeen, eighteen,
Maids a-waiting;
Nineteen, twenty,
My plate's empty.

## COCK-A-DOODLE-DO!

Cock-a-doodle-do!
My dame has lost her shoe,
My master's lost his fiddle-stick
And knows not what to do.

Cock-a-doodle-do!
What is my dame to do?
Till master finds his fiddle-stick,
She'll dance without her shoe.

## PAIRS OR PEARS

Twelve pairs hanging high,
Twelve knights riding by,
Each knight took a pear,
And yet left a dozen there.

## BELLEISLE

At the siege of Belleisle
I was there all the while,
All the while, all the while,
At the siege of Belleisle.

DAPPLE-GRAY

## OLD KING COLE

Old King Cole
Was a merry old soul,
And a merry old soul was he;
    He called for his pipe,
    And he called for his bowl,
And he called for his fiddlers three!
And every fiddler, he had a fine
        fiddle,
    And a very fine fiddle had he.
"Twee tweedle dee, tweedle dee,"
        went the fiddlers.
    Oh, there's none so rare
    As can compare
With King Cole and his fiddlers
        three.

## SEE, SEE

See, see! What shall I see?
A horse's head where his tail
        should be.

## DAPPLE-GRAY

had a little pony,
    His name was Dapple-Gray,
lent him to a lady,
    To ride a mile away.
She whipped him, she slashed him,
    She rode him through the mire;
would not lend my pony now
    For all the lady's hire.

## A WELL

As round as an apple, as deep as a
        cup,
And all the king's horses can't fill
    it up.

## COFFEE AND TEA

Molly, my sister and I fell out,
And what do you think it was all
        about?
She loved coffee and I loved tea,
And that was the reason we couldn't
        agree.

## PUSSY-CAT MEW

Pussy-cat Mew jumped over a coal,
And in her best petticoat burnt a
        great hole.
Poor Pussy's weeping, she'll have
        no more milk
Until her best petticoat's mended
        with silk.

## A COCK AND BULL STORY

The cock's on the housetop blowing
    his horn;
The bull's in the barn a-threshing
    of corn;
The maids in the meadows are
    making of hay;
The ducks in the river are swim-
    ming away.

## FOR BABY

You shall have an apple,
YOU shall have a plum,
You shall have a rattle,
When papa comes home.

## THE LITTLE GIRL WITH A CURL

There was a little girl who had a little
    curl
Right in the middle of her forehead;
When she was good, she was very,
    very good,
And when she was bad she was
    horrid.

## DREAMS

Friday night's dream, on Saturday
    told,
Is sure to come true, be it never so
    old.

## OVER THE WATER

Over the water, and over the sea,
And over the water to Charley,
I'll have none of your nasty beef,
Nor I'll have none of your barley;
But I'll have some of your very best
     flour
To make a white cake for my
     Charley.

## CANDLE-SAVING

To make your candles last for aye,
You wives and maids give ear-O!
To put them out's the only way,
Says honest John Boldero.

## MYSELF

As I walked by myself,
And talked to myself,
    Myself said unto me:
"Look to thyself,
Take care of thyself,
    For nobody cares for thee."

I answered myself,
And said to myself
    In the selfsame repartee:
"Look to thyself,
Or not look to thyself,
    The selfsame thing will be."

LADYBIRD

## OLD GRIMES

Old Grimes is dead, that good old
man,
We ne'er shall see him more;
He used to wear a long brown coat
All buttoned down before.

## A WEEK OF BIRTHDAYS

Monday's child is fair of face,
Tuesday's child is full of grace,
Wednesday's child is full of woe,
Thursday's child has far to go,
Friday's child is loving and giving,
Saturday's child works hard for its
living,
But the child that's born on the
Sabbath day
Is bonny and blithe, and good and
gay.

## FEARS AND TEARS

Tommy's tears and Mary's fears
Will make them old before their
years.

## THE KILKENNY CATS

There were once two cats of
Kilkenny.
Each thought there was one cat too
many;
So they fought and they fit,
And they scratched and they bit,
Till, excepting their nails,
And the tips of their tails,
Instead of two cats, there weren't
any.

## A CHIMNEY

Black within and red without;
Four corners round about.

## LADYBIRD

Ladybird, ladybird, fly away home!
Your house is on fire, your children
all gone,
All but one, and her name is Ann,
And she crept under the pudding
pan.

## THE MAN WHO HAD NAUGHT

There was a man and he had naught,
   And robbers came to rob him;
He crept up to the chimney pot,
   And then they thought they
      had him.

But he got down on t'other side,
   And then they could not find
      him;
He ran fourteen miles in fifteen days,
   And never looked behind him.

## THE TAILORS AND THE SNAIL

Four and Twenty tailors
   Went to kill a snail;
The best man among them
   Durst not touch her tail;
She put out her horns
   Like a little Kyloe cow.
Run, tailors, run, or
   She'll kill you all e'en now.

## AROUND THE GREEN GRAVEL

Around the green gravel the grass
   grows green,
And all the pretty maids are plain
   to be seen;
Wash them with milk, and clothe
   them with silk,
And write their names with a pen
   and ink.

## INTERY, MINTERY

Intery, mintery, cutery corn,
Apple seed and apple thorn;
Wire, brier, limber-lock,
Five geese in a flock,
Sit and sing by a spring,
O-u-t, and in again.

## CAESAR'S SONG

Bow-wow-wow!
Whose dog art thou?
Little Tom Tinker's dog,
Bow-wow-wow!

# AS I WAS GOING ALONG

As I was going along, along,
A-singing a comical song, song, song,
The lane that I went was so long,
    long, long,
And the song that I sang was so
    long, long, long,
And so I went singing along.

## HECTOR PROTECTOR

Hector Protector was dressed all in
    green;
Hector Protector was sent to the
    Queen.
The Queen did not like him,
No more did the King;
So Hector Protector was sent back
    again.

## BILLY, BILLY

"Billy, Billy, come and play,
While the sun shines bright as day."

"Yes, my Polly, so I will,
For I love to please you still."

"Billy, Billy, have you seen
Sam and Betsy on the green?"

"Yes, my Poll, I saw them pass,
Skipping o'er the new-mown grass."

"Billy, Billy, come along,
And I will sing a pretty song."

## ROCK-A-BYE, BABY

Rock-a-bye, baby, thy cradle is green;
Father's a nobleman, mother's a
    queen;
And Betty's a lady, and wears a
    gold ring;
And Johnny's a drummer, and
    drums for the king.

## THE MAN IN THE WILDERNESS

The man in the wilderness
    Asked me
How many strawberries
    Grew in the sea.
I answered him
    As I thought good,
As many as red herrings
    Grew in the wood.

## LITTLE JACK HORNER

Little Jack Horner
Sat in the corner,
    Eating of Christmas pie:
He put in his thumb,
And pulled out a plum,
    And said, "What a good boy
      am I!"

## THE BIRD SCARER

Away, birds, away!
Take a little and leave a little,
And do not come again;
For if you do,
I will shoot you through,
And there will be an end of you.

## MARY, MARY, QUITE CONTRARY

Mary, Mary, quite contrary,
    How does your garden grow?
Silver bells and cockle-shells,
    And pretty maids all of a row.

## BESSY BELL AND MARY GRAY

Bessy Bell and Mary Gray,
    They were two bonny lasses;
They built their house upon the lea,
    And covered it with rushes.

Bessy kept the garden gate,
    And Mary kept the pantry;
Bessy always had to wait,
    While Mary lived in plenty.

MARY, MARY, QUITE CONTRARY

## NEEDLES AND PINS

Needles and pins, needles and pins,

When a man marries his trouble begins.

## PUSSY-CAT AND THE DUMPLINGS

Pussy-cat ate the dumplings, the dumplings,

    Pussy-cat ate the dumplings.

Mamma stood by, and cried, "Oh, fie!

    Why did you eat the dumplings?"

## DANCE, THUMBKIN DANCE

Dance, Thumbkin, dance;

    *(keep the thumb in motion*

Dance, ye merrymen, everyone.

    *(all the fingers in motion*

For Thumbkin, he can dance alone,

    *(the thumb alone moving*

Thumbkin, he can dance alone.

    *(the thumb alone moving*

Dance, Foreman, dance,

    *(the first finger moving*

Dance, ye merrymen, everyone.

    *(all moving*

But Foreman, he can dance alone,

    *(the first finger moving*

Foreman, he can dance alone.

    *(the first finger moving*

Dance, Longman, dance,

    *(the second finger moving*

Dance, ye merrymen, everyone.

    *(all moving*

For Longman, he can dance alone,

    *(the second finger moving*

Longman, he can dance alone.

    *(the second finger moving*

Dance, Ringman, dance,

    *(the third finger moving*

Dance, ye merrymen, dance.

    *(all moving*

But Ringman cannot dance alone,

    *(the third finger moving*

Ringman, he cannot dance alone.

    *(the third finger moving*

Dance, Littleman, dance,

    *(the fourth finger moving*

Dance, ye merrymen, dance.

    *(all moving*

But Littleman, he can dance alone,

    *(the fourth finger moving*

Littleman, he can dance alone.

    *(the fourth finger moving*

## THE LITTLE BIRD

Once I saw a little bird
    Come hop, hop, hop;
So I cried, "Little bird,
    Will you stop, stop, stop?"

And was going to the window
    To say, "How do you do?"
But he shook his little tail,
    And far away he flew.

## BIRDS OF A FEATHER

Birds of a feather flock together,
    And so will pigs and swine;
Rats and mice will have their choice,
    And so will I have mine.

## MARY'S CANARY

Mary had a pretty bird,
    Feathers bright and yellow,
Slender legs—upon my word
    He was a pretty fellow!

The sweetest note he always sung,
    Which much delighted Mary.
She often, where the cage was hung,
    Sat hearing her canary.

# THE DUSTY MILLER

Margaret wrote a letter,
Sealed it with her finger,
Threw it in the dam
For the dusty miller.
Dusty was his coat,
Dusty was the siller,
Dusty was the kiss
I'd from the dusty miller.
If I had my pockets
Full of gold and siller,
I would give it all
To my dusty miller.

## A STAR

Higher  than  a  house,  higher
than a tree.
Oh! whatever can that be?

## THE GREEDY MAN

The greedy man is he who sits
And bites bits out of plates,
Or else takes up an almanac
And gobbles all the dates.

## THE TEN O'CLOCK
SCHOLAR

A diller, a dollar, a ten o'clock scholar!
What makes you come so soon?
You used to come at ten o'clock,
But now you come at noon.

THE TEN O'CLOCK SCHOLAR

## COCK-A-DOODLE-DO

Oh, my pretty cock, oh, my handsome cock,
    I pray you, do not crow before day,
And your comb shall be made of the very
        beaten gold,
    And your wings of the silver so gray.

### AN ICICLE

Lives in winter,
Dies in summer,
And grows with its roots upward!

### A SHIP'S NAIL

Over the water,
And under the water,
And always with its head down.

## THE OLD WOMAN OF LEEDS

There was an old woman of Leeds,
Who spent all her time in good
        deeds;
    She worked for the poor
    Till her fingers were sore,
This pious old woman of Leeds!

## THE BOY IN THE BARN

A little boy went into a barn,
    And lay down on some hay.
An owl came out, and flew about,
    And the little boy ran away.

## SUNSHINE

Hick-a-more, Hack-a-more,
On the King's kitchen door,
All the King's horses,
And all the King's men,
Couldn't drive Hick-a-more,
        Hack-a-more,
Off the King's kitchen door.

## WILLY, WILLY

Willy, Willy Wilkin
Kissed the maids a-milking,
        Fa, la, la!
And with his merry daffing
He set them all a-laughing,
        Ha, ha, ha!

## THE QUARREL

My little old man and I fell out;
I'll tell you what 'twas all about,—
I had money and he had none,
And that's the way the noise begun.

## THE PUMPKIN-EATER

Peter, Peter, pumpkin-eater,
Had a wife and couldn't keep her;
He put her in a pumpkin shell,
And there he kept her very well.

## TONGS

Long legs, crooked thighs,
Little head, and no eyes.

## JACK JINGLE

Little Jack Jingle,
He used to live single;
But when he got tired of this
    kind of life,
He left off being single and
    lived with his wife.
Now what do you think of
    little Jack Jingle?
Before he was married he used
    to live single.

PETER, PETER, PUMPKIN-EATER

## THAT'S ALL

There was an old woman sat spinning
And that's the first beginning;

She had a calf,
And that's half;

She took it by the tail,
And threw it over the wall,
And that's all!

## SHOEING

Shoe the colt,
Shoe the colt,
Shoe the wild mare;
Here a nail,
There a nail,
Yet she goes bare.

## BETTY BLUE

Little Betty Blue
Lost her holiday shoe;
What shall little Betty do?
Give her another
To match the other
And then she'll walk upon two.

# BEDTIME

The Man in the Moon looked
    out of the moon,
    Looked out of the moon
    and said,
"'Tis time for all children
    on the earth
    To think about getting to bed!"

## DANCE, LITTLE BABY

Dance, little Baby, dance up high!
Never mind, Baby, Mother is by.
Crow and caper, caper and crow,
There, little Baby, there you go!
Up to the ceiling, down to the
    ground,
Backwards and forwards, round
    and round;
Dance, little Baby and Mother
    will sing,
With the merry coral, ding, ding,
    ding!

## MY LITTLE MAID

High diddle doubt, my candle's
    out
    My little maid is not at home;
Saddle my hog and bridle my
    dog,
    And fetch my little maid
    home.

## FOR WANT OF A NAIL

For want of a nail, the shoe was lost;
For want of the shoe, the horse was
    lost;
For want of the horse, the rider was
    lost;
For want of the rider, the battle was
    lost;
For want of the battle, the kingdom
    was lost,
And all for the want of a horseshoe
    nail.

## THE CROOKED SIXPENCE

There was a crooked man, and he
    went a crooked mile,
He found a crooked sixpence be
    side a crooked stile;
He bought a crooked cat, which
    caught a crooked mouse,
And they all lived together in a
    little crooked house.

## THIS IS THE WAY

This is the way the ladies ride,
    Tri, tre, tre, tree,
    Tri, tre, tre, tree!
This is the way the ladies ride,
    Tri, tre, tre, tre, tri-tre-tre-tree

This is the way the gentlemen ride
    Gallop-a-trot,
    Gallop-a-trot!
This is the way the gentlemen ride
    Gallop-a-gallop-a-trot!

This is the way the farmers ride,
    Hobbledy-hoy,
    Hobbledy-hoy!
This is the way the farmers ride,
    Hobbledy-hobbledy-hoy!

## PEASE PORRIDGE

Pease porridge hot,
    Pease porridge cold,
Pease porridge in the pot,
    Nine days old.
Some like it hot,
    Some like it cold,
Some like it in the pot,
    Nine days old.

## RING A RING O' ROSES

Ring a ring o' roses,
A pocketful of posies.
Tisha! Tisha!
We all fall down.

PEASE PORRIDGE HOT

## DUCKS AND DRAKES

A duck and a drake,
And a halfpenny cake,
With a penny to pay the old baker.

A hop and a scotch
Is another notch,
Slitherum, slatherum, take her.

## THE DONKEY

Donkey, donkey, old and gray,
Ope your mouth and gently bray;
Lift your ears and blow your horn,
To wake the world this sleepy
morn.

## IF

If all the world were apple pie,
And all the sea were ink,
And all the trees were bread and
cheese,
What should we have for drink?

# THE BELLS

"You **owe me five** shillings,"
Say the bells of St. Helen's.

"When will you pay me?"
Say the bells of Old Bailey.

"When I grow rich,"
Say the bells of Shoreditch.

"When will that be?"
Say the bells of Stepney.

"I do not know,"
Says the great Bell of Bow.

"Two sticks in an apple,"
Ring the bells of Whitechapel.

"Halfpence and farthings,"
Say the bells of St. Martin's.

"Kettles and pans,"
Say the bells of St. Ann's.

"Brickbats and tiles,"
Say the bells of St. Giles.

"Old shoes and slippers,"
Say the bells of St. Peter's.

"Pokers and tongs,"
Say the bells of St. John's.

## LITTLE GIRL AND QUEEN

"Little girl, little girl, where have
    you been?"
"Gathering roses to give to the
    Queen."
"Little girl, little girl, what gave
    she you?"
"She gave me a diamond as big as
    my shoe."

## THE KING OF FRANCE

The King of France went up the
    hill,
    With twenty thousand men;
The King of France came down the
    hill,
    And ne'er went up again.

THE TARTS

## PETER PIPER

Peter Piper picked a peck of
    pickled peppers;
A peck of pickled peppers Peter
    Piper picked.
If Peter Piper picked a peck of
    pickled peppers,
Where's the peck of pickled peppers
    Peter Piper picked?

## ONE TO TEN

1, 2, 3, 4, 5!
I caught a hare alive;
6, 7, 8, 9, 10!
I let her go again.

## AN EQUAL

Read my riddle, I pray.
What God never sees,
What the king seldom sees,
What we see every day.

## THE TARTS

The Queen of Hearts,
    She made some tarts,
All on a summer's day;
    The Knave of Hearts,
    He stole the tarts,
And took them clean away.

    The King of Hearts
    Called for the tarts,
And beat the Knave full sore;
    The Knave of Hearts
    Brought back the tarts,
And vowed he'd steal no more.

## WHAT ARE LITTLE BOYS MADE OF?

What are little boys made of, made
　of?
What are little boys made of?
"Snaps and snails, and puppy-dogs'
　tails;
And that's what little boys are
　made of."

What are little girls made of, made
　of?
What are little girls made of?
"Sugar and spice, and all that's
　nice;
And that's what little girls are
　made of."

## COME, LET'S TO BED

"To bed! To bed!"
　Says Sleepy-head;
"Tarry awhile," says Slow;
"Put on the pan,"
　Says Greedy Nan;
　"We'll sup before we go."

## LITTLE MAID

"Little maid, pretty maid, whither
　goest thou?"
"Down in the forest to milk my
　cow."
'Shall I go with thee?"　"No, not
　now;
When I send for thee, then come
　thou."

So I went into Darlington, that
    pretty little town,
And there I bought a petticoat, a
    cloak, and a gown.

I went into the woods and built
    me a kirk,
And all the birds of the air, they
    helped me to work.

The hawk with his long claws
    pulled down the stone,
The dove with her rough bill
    brought me them home.

The parrot was the clergyman, the
    peacock was the clerk,
The bullfinch played the organ, —
    we made merry work.

## BANDY LEGS

As I was going to sell my eggs
I met a man with bandy legs,
Bandy legs and crooked toes;
I tripped up his heels, and he
    fell on his nose.

## THE GIRL AND THE
## BIRDS

When I was a little girl, about
    seven years old,
I had n't got a petticoat, to cover
    me from the cold.

## A PIG

As I went to Bonner,
I met a pig
Without a wig
Upon my word and honor.

## JENNY WREN

As little Jenny Wren
    Was sitting by her shed.
She waggled with her tail,
    And nodded with her head.
She waggled with her tail,
    And nodded with her head,
As little Jenny Wren
    Was sitting by the shed.

## LITTLE TOM TUCKER

Little Tom Tucker
    Sings for his supper.
What shall he eat?
    White bread and butter.
How will he cut it
    Without e'er a knife?
How will he be married
    Without e'er a wife?

LITTLE TOM TUCKER

## WHERE ARE YOU GOING, MY PRETTY MAID

"Where are you going, my pretty maid?"

"I'm going a-milking, sir," she said.

"May I go with you, my pretty maid?"

"You're kindly welcome, sir," she said.

"What is your father, my pretty maid?"

"My father's a farmer, sir," she said.

"What is your fortune, my pretty maid?"

"My face is my fortune, sir," she said.

"Then I can't marry you, my pretty maid."

"Nobody asked you, sir," she said.

## THE OLD WOMAN OF GLOUCESTER

There was an old woman of Gloucester,

Whose parrot two guineas it cost her,

But its tongue never ceasing,

Was vastly displeasing

To the talkative woman of Gloucester.

## MULTIPLICATION IS VEXATION

Multiplication is vexation,
　　Division is as bad;
The Rule of Three doth puzzle me,
　　And Practice drives me mad.

## LITTLE KING BOGGEN

Little King Boggen, he built a fine
　　hall,
Pie-crust and pastry-crust, that was
　　the wall;
The windows were made of black
　　puddings and white,
And slated with pan-cakes,—you
　　ne'er saw the like!

## WHISTLE

"Whistle, daughter, whistle;
　　Whistle, daughter dear."
"I cannot whistle, mammy,
　　I cannot whistle clear."
"Whistle, daughter, whistle;
　　Whistle for a pound."
"I cannot whistle, mammy,
　　I cannot make a sound."

## BELL HORSES

Bell horses, bell horses, what
　　time of day?
One o'clock, two o'clock, three
　　and away.

## TAFFY

Taffy was a Welshman, Taffy was
　　a thief,
Taffy came to my house and stole a
　　piece of beef;
I went to Taffy's house, Taffy was
　　not home;
Taffy came to my house and stole a
　　marrow-bone.

I went to Taffy's house, Taffy was
　　not in;
Taffy came to my house and stole a
　　silver pin;
I went to Taffy's house, Taffy was
　　in bed,
I took up the marrow-bone and
　　flung it at his head.

## YOUNG ROGER AND DOLLY

Young Roger came tapping at
  Dolly's window,
    Thumpaty, thumpaty, thump!

He asked for admittance; she
    answered him "No!"
  Frumpaty, frumpaty, frump!

"No, no, Roger, no! as you came
    you may go!"
  Stumpaty, stumpaty, stump!

## THE ROBIN

The north wind doth blow,
And we shall have snow,
And what will poor robin do then,
          Poor thing?
He'll sit in a barn,
And keep himself warm,
And hide his head under his wing,
          Poor thing!

## THE OLD WOMAN OF
## HARROW

There was an old woman of
    Harrow,
Who visited in a wheelbarrow;
    And her servant before,
    Knocked loud at each door,
To announce the old woman of
    Harrow.

YOUNG ROGER AND DOLLY

## THE COACHMAN

Up at Piccadilly, oh!
 The coachman takes his stand,
And when he meets a pretty girl
 He takes her by the hand;
Whip away forever, oh!
 Drive away so clever, oh!
All the way to Bristol, oh!
 He drives her four-in-hand.

## THERE WAS AN OLD WOMAN

There was an old woman who lived
 in a shoe.
She had so many children she
 didn't know what to do.
She gave them some broth without
 any bread.
She whipped them all soundly and
 put them to bed.

## THE PIPER AND HIS COW

There was a piper had a cow,
 And he had naught to give her;
He pulled out his pipes and played
  her a tune,
 And bade the cow consider.

The cow considered very well,
 And gave the piper a penny,
And bade him play the other tune,
 "Corn rigs are bonny."

## THE MAN OF DERBY

A little old man of Derby,
How do you think he served me?
He took away my bread and cheese,
And that is how he served me.

## A THORN

I went to the wood and got it;
I sat me down to look for it
And brought it home because I
      couldn't find it.

## THE OLD WOMAN OF SURREY

There was an old woman in Surrey,
Who was morn, noon, and night
      in a hurry;
      Called her husband a fool,
      Drove the children to school,
The worrying old woman of Surrey.

## THE LITTLE MOUSE

I have seen you, little mouse,

Running all about the house,

Through the hole your little eye

In the wainscot peeping sly,

Hoping soon some crumbs to steal,

To make quite a hearty meal.

Look before you venture out,

See if pussy is about.

If she's gone, you'll quickly run

To the larder for some fun;

Round about the dishes creep,

Taking into each a peep,

To choose the daintiest that's there,

Spoiling things you do not care.

## BOY AND GIRL

There was a little boy and a
    little girl
    Lived in an alley;
Says the little boy to the little
    girl,
    "Shall I, oh, shall I?"
Says the little girl to the little
    boy,
    "What shall we do?"
Says the little boy to the little
    girl,
    "I will kiss you."

## WHEN

When I was
    a bachelor
I lived by
    myself;
And all the
    bread and
    cheese I got
I laid up on the
    shelf.

The rats and the mice
    They made such a strife,
I was forced to go to London
    To buy me a wife.

The streets were so bad,
    And the lanes were so narrow,
I was forced to bring my wife home
    In a wheelbarrow.

The wheelbarrow broke,
    And my wife had a fall;
Down came wheelbarrow,
    Little wife and all.

WHEN I WAS A BACHELOR

## SING, SING

Sing, sing, what shall I
    sing?
Cat's run away with the
    pudding-string!
Do, do, what shall I
    do?
The cat has bitten it
    quite in two.

## LONDON BRIDGE

London Bridge is broken down,
Dance over my Lady Lee;
London Bridge is broken down,
With a gay lady.

How shall we build it up again?
Dance over my Lady Lee;
How shall we build it up again?
With a gay lady.

Build it up with silver and gold,
Dance over my Lady Lee;
Build it up with silver and gold,
With a gay lady.

Silver and gold will be stole away,
Dance over my Lady Lee;
Silver and gold will be stole away,
With a gay lady.

Build it up with iron and steel,
Dance over my Lady Lee;
Build it up with iron and steel,
With a gay lady.

Iron and steel will bend and bow,
Dance over my Lady Lee;
Iron and steel will bend and bow,
With a gay lady.

Build it up with wood and clay,
Dance over my Lady Lee;
Build it up with wood and clay,
With a gay lady.

Wood and clay will wash away,
Dance over my Lady Lee;
Wood and clay will wash away,
With a gay lady.

Build it up with stone so strong,
Dance over my Lady Lee;
Huzza! 'twill last for ages long,
With a gay lady.

## MARCH WINDS

March winds and April showers
Bring forth May flowers.

## THE LOST SHOE

Doodle doodle doo,
The Princess lost her shoe:
Her Highness hopped,—
The fiddler stopped,
Not knowing what to do.

## HOT CODLINS

There was a little woman, as I've
been told,
Who was not very young, nor yet
very old;
Now this little woman her living got
By selling codlins, hot, hot, hot!

## THE BALLOON

"What is the news of the day,
Good neighbor, I pray?"
"They say the balloon
Is gone up to the moon!"

## A CHERRY

As I went through the garden gap,
Who should I meet but Dick Red-
cap!
A stick in his hand, a stone in his
throat,—
If you'll tell me this riddle, I'll
give you a groat.

## SWAN

Swan, swan, over the sea;
　　Swim, swan, swim!
Swan, swan, back again;
　　Well swum, swan!

## THREE STRAWS

Three straws on a staff
Would make a baby cry and laugh.

## THE MAN OF TOBAGO

There was an old man of Tobago
Who lived on rice, gruel, and sago,
　　Till much to his bliss,
　　His physician said this:
"To a leg, sir, of mutton, you may
　　go."

## DING, DONG, BELL

Ding, dong, bell,
Pussy's in the well!
Who put her in?
Little Tommy Lin.

Who pulled her out?
Little Johnny Stout.
What a naughty boy was that,
To try to drown poor pussy-cat.
Who never did him any harm,
But killed the mice in his father's
　　barn!

## A SUNSHINY SHOWER

A sunshiny shower
Won't last half an hour.

The mischievous raven flew laugh-
ing away,
Bumpety, bumpety, bump!
And vowed he would serve them
the same the next day,
Lumpety, lumpety lump!

## CHRISTMAS

Christmas is coming, the geese are
getting fat,
Please to put a penny in an old
man's hat;
If you haven't got a penny a
ha'penny will do,
If you haven't got a ha'penny, God
bless you.

## THE FARMER AND THE RAVEN

A farmer went trotting upon his
gray mare,
Bumpety, bumpety, bump!
With his daughter behind him so
rosy and fair,
Lumpety, lumpety, lump!

A raven cried croak! and they all
tumbled down,
Bumpety, bumpety, bump!
The mare broke her knees, and the
farmer his crown,
Lumpety, lumpety, lump!

## WILLY BOY

"Willy boy, Willy boy, where are
    you going?
I will go with you, if that I
    may."
"I'm going to the meadow to
    see them a-mowing,
I'm going to help them to make
    the hay."

## POLLY AND SUKEY

Polly, put the kettle on,
Polly, put the kettle on,
Polly, put the kettle on,
    And let's drink tea.

Sukey, take it off again,
Sukey, take it off again,
Sukey, take it off again,
    They're all gone away.

## THE DEATH AND BURIAL
## OF POOR COCK ROBIN

Who killed Cock Robin?
"I," said the sparrow,
"With my little bow and arrow,
I killed Cock Robin."

Who saw him die?
"I," said the fly,
"With my little eye,
I saw him die."

Who caught his blood?
"I," said the fish,
"With my little dish,
I caught his blood."

Who'll make his shroud?
"I," said the beetle,
"With my thread and needle.
I'll make his shroud."

Who'll carry the torch?
"I," said the linnet,
"I'll come in a minute,
I'll carry the torch."

Who'll be the clerk?
"I," said the lark,
"If it's not in the dark,
I'll be the clerk."

Who'll dig his grave?
"I," said the owl,
"With my spade and trowel
I'll dig his grave."

Who'll be the parson?
"I," said the rook,
"With my little book,
I'll be the parson."

Who'll be chief mourner?
"I," said the dove,
"I mourn for my love,
I'll be chief mourner."

Who'll sing a psalm?
"I," said the thrush,
"As I sit in a bush.
I'll sing a psalm."

Who'll carry the coffin?
"I," said the kite,
"If it's not in the night,
I'll carry the coffin."

Who'll toll the bell?
"I," said the bull,
"Because I can pull,
I'll toll the bell."

All the birds of the air
Fell sighing and sobbing,
When they heard the bell toll
For poor Cock Robin.

## THE MOUSE AND THE CLOCK

Hickory, dickory, dock!
The mouse ran up the clock;
The clock struck one,
And down he run,
Hickory, dickory, dock!

THE BUNCH OF BLUE RIBBONS

# THE BUNCH OF BLUE RIBBONS

Oh, dear, what can the matter be?
Oh, dear, what can the matter be?
Oh, dear, what can the matter be?
    Johnny's so long at the fair.

He promised he'd buy me a bunch
    of blue ribbons,
He promised he'd buy me a bunch
    of blue ribbons,
He promised he'd buy me a bunch
    of blue ribbons,
    To tie up my bonny brown
    hair.

## HOT-CROSS BUNS

Hot-cross Buns!
Hot cross Buns!
One a penny, two a penny,
Hot-cross Buns!
Hot-cross Buns!
Hot-cross Buns!
If ye have no daughters,
Give them to your sons.

## BOBBY SHAFTOE

Bobby Shaftoe's gone to sea,
With silver buckles on his knee:
He'll come back and marry me,
    Pretty Bobby Shaftoe!
Bobby Shaftoe's fat and fair,
Combing down his yellow hair;
He's my love for evermore,
    Pretty Bobby Shaftoe.

## THE WOMAN OF EXETER

There dwelt an old woman at Exeter;
When visitors came it sore vexed her,
    So for fear they should eat,
    She locked up all her meat,
This stingy old woman of Exeter.

## SNEEZING

If you sneeze on Monday, you
    sneeze for danger;
Sneeze on a Tuesday, kiss a
    stranger;
Sneeze on a Wednesday, sneeze for
    a letter;
Sneeze on a Thursday, something
    better.
Sneeze on a Friday, sneeze for
    sorrow;
Sneeze on a Saturday, joy to-
    morrow.

## PUSSY-CAT BY THE FIRE

Pussy-cat sits by the fire;
    How can she be fair?
In walks the little dog;
    Says: "Pussy, are you there?
How do you do, Mistress Pussy?
    Mistress Pussy, how d'ye do?"
"I thank you kindly, little dog,
    I fare as well as you!"

## WHEN THE SNOW IS ON THE GROUND

The little robin grieves
    When the snow is on the ground
For the trees have no leaves,
    And no berries can be found
The air is cold, the worms are hid
    For robin here what can be
    done?
Let's strow around some crumbs of
    bread,
    And then he'll live till snow is
    gone.